www.houghtonmifflinbooks.com

The text of this book is set in Leawood.
The illustrations are watercolor.

Library of Congress Cataloging-in-Publication Data

Gregorich, Barbara.
Waltur buys a pig in a poke and other stories/
by Barbara Gregorich ; illustrated by Kristin Sorra.
p. cm.
Summary: Two bears, Waltur and Darwin, learn from their
friend Matilda such lessons as "do not buy a pig in a poke"
and "you can lead a horse to water, but you can't make him drink."
ISBN 0-618-47306-8 (hc)
[1. Bears—Fiction. 2. Animals—Fiction.
3. Idioms—Fiction.] I. Sorra, Kristin, ill. II. Title.
PZ7.G8613Wal 2006
[Fic]—dc22
2004020564

ISBN-13: 978-0618-47306-9

Manufactured in China
SNP 10 9 8 7 6 5 4 3 2 1

WALTUR
BUYS A PIG IN A POKE
AND OTHER STORIES

For Rosalynne - B.G.

For Abuela - K.S.

WALTUR
BUYS A PIG IN A POKE
AND OTHER STORIES

by Barbara Gregorich
Illustrated by Kristin Sorra

Houghton Mifflin Company
Boston 2006

CONTENTS

WALTUR

BUYS A PIG IN A POKE

1

Waltur Wants a Pet

Waltur scratched his fur.
He patted his paws.
He clicked his claws.

"You are thinking," said Matilda.
"What about?"

"A pet," said Waltur.
"I want a pet."

"Why?" asked Matilda.
"You have me."

"You are too smart to be a pet," said Waltur.
"Thank you," said Matilda.

"You don't come when I call," said Waltur.
"You never fetch my slippers.
 And you never do tricks," he said.
"I want a pet who does what I say."

"Pets aren't like that," said Matilda.

Just then, someone pounded on the door.
It was Darwin.
"There's a fair in the forest," said Darwin.
"There are rides and games and animals."
Waltur clapped his paws.

"Are there pigs?" he asked.
"I think so," said Darwin.
"Good," Waltur said.
"I will buy a pig for a pet."

"A pig will come when I call," said Waltur.
"It will fetch my slippers.
I will teach it tricks," he said.

"Pigs are dirty," said Darwin.
"Pigs are smart," said Matilda.

2
A Pig in a Poke

The three friends went to the fair.
"I will go on rides," said Darwin.
"I will play games," said Matilda.
"And I will buy a pig," said Waltur.

"Be careful," said Matilda.
"Do not buy a pig in a poke."

"What's a poke?" asked Darwin.
"A poke is a bag," Matilda answered.
"You cannot see through a bag.
You should not buy what
you cannot see," she said.

Matilda went to play games.
Darwin went to go on rides.
Waltur went to buy a pet.

"Want to buy a pig?" asked a skunk.
Waltur saw that the pig was in a big bag.
Waltur scratched his fur and thought hard.
"No," he said at last.
"I know better than to buy a pig in a poke."

"Want to buy a pig?" asked a bobcat.
Waltur saw that the pig was in a big sack.
"No," said Waltur.
"I know better than to buy a pig in a poke."

"Want to buy a pig?"
asked a fox.
Waltur saw that the pig
was in a big, big box.

"Is it a smart pig?"
asked Waltur.
"It is very smart,"
said the fox.

"Can it fetch slippers?" asked Waltur.
"Sure," said the fox.
"Can I teach it tricks?" asked Waltur.
"Why not?"
said the fox.
"I'll buy it,"
said Waltur.

3
The Pig in the Box

Waltur pushed the big,
big box home.
Matilda and Darwin
helped.
"What is in the box?"
huffed Darwin.
"My new pet,"
puffed Waltur.
"What does it look like?"
huffed Matilda.

"I don't know yet,"
said Waltur.
"But a box is
not a bag.
I did not buy
a pig in a poke."
"We will see,"
said Matilda.

When he got home,
Waltur opened the box.
Out jumped the pig.
It was very big.
It was very, very dirty.

"Hot dog!" said the pig. "Home!"

The pig ran through the house.
It broke a lamp.
It smashed a table.
It ate Waltur's lunch.

"Hot dog!" said the pig.
It sat in Waltur's chair.

"Bring me the paper," said the pig.
"No!" said Waltur.

"Fetch me some slippers," said the pig.
"No!" shouted Waltur.

"Do some tricks," said the pig.
"Grrrrr," growled Waltur.
"Oink," oinked the pig.

4
A Perfect Pet

"You are not what I wanted,"
  said Waltur.
"Too bad," said the pig.
"I wish I had seen you before I
  bought you," said Waltur.
"I was in a box," said the pig.
"You couldn't see me.
  You bought a pig in a poke.
  Oink, oink!"

"What am I going to do?"
  asked Waltur.
He sat on the floor
  and thought.

"More food!" said the pig.
 Darwin gave the pig a hot dog.
"Good bear," said the pig.

"Bring me the paper," said the pig.
 Darwin brought the paper.
"Fetch me some slippers," said the pig.
 Darwin fetched some slippers.
 They were Waltur's slippers.

"Good bear," said the pig.
The pig patted Darwin on the head.
"What a wonderful pet," said Darwin.

"Wonderful?" asked Matilda.
"Yes, wonderful!" Darwin said.
"I wish I had a pet like this."

Waltur stood up.
"You may have my pig," he said.
"Really?" asked Darwin.
"Hot dog!" said the pig.

"Yes," said Waltur.
"It is your pig now.
  The pig can have my slippers, too,"
  said Waltur.
"Hot dog!" said the pig.

"Thank you so much," said Darwin.
"Let's go home," said the pig.
  The pig and Darwin went home.

Waltur cleaned up his house.
Matilda used the box to make a table.
They made a new lunch and ate it.

"I guess I should have looked inside the box," said Waltur.
"I guess so," said Matilda.

"Someday I will buy another pet," said Waltur.
"What about you?" he asked.
"Do you want a pet?"

"No," said Matilda.
"I have you."

PIG :
⬆ THIS SNOUT
UP

WALTUR

COUNTS HIS CHICKENS BEFORE THEY ARE HATCHED

1

Waltur Wants Honey

Waltur and Matilda walked in the woods.
They saw a sign: HONEY 4 SALE.
Waltur licked his lips.
"I want honey," he said.
He licked his lips again.

But Waltur did not have enough money.
"I must get more money," he said.

They saw another sign: EGGS 4 SALE.
"I have a plan," said Waltur.
"What is your plan?" asked Matilda.

"I will buy eggs," said Waltur.

"The eggs will hatch into chickens.
 I will sell the chickens."

 Waltur clapped his paws.
"I will get a lot of money," he said.
"And then I will buy honey."

"Don't be so sure," Matilda said.
"Don't count your chickens before
 they are hatched."

"But I want to count them now," said Waltur.
"Then I will know how much honey I can buy."

 Matilda rubbed her snout.

 Waltur bought many eggs.
 He and Matilda walked home with the eggs.
 On the way, they saw a chicken.
 It was a hen.
"Hey, hen," said Waltur. "Come with me."
"*Cluck,*" said the hen.

2
Waltur Does Not Count

Matilda put a box in the backyard.
She put straw in to make a nest.
Waltur put all the eggs into the nest.
The hen sat on the eggs.
"*Cluck,*" said the hen.

Waltur started to count the eggs.
"One, two, three," he said.
Then he stopped.
"No," he said.
"I should not count my chickens before
  they are hatched."

"That is right," said Matilda.
"You might get a lot of chickens," she said.
"Or you might get none."

"You are wrong," said Waltur.
"I counted three eggs before I stopped.
 I will get at least three chickens."

Matilda rubbed her snout.

The next morning, Darwin came to visit.
"You have a lot of eggs," he said.
"I see five, six, seven—"
"Stop!" shouted Waltur.
"Do not count!"

"All of the eggs will become chickens,"
 said Waltur.
"I will sell the chickens for money.
 Then I will buy a lot of honey," he said.

Waltur and Darwin went indoors.
Waltur wanted many, many jars of honey.
He wanted one jar of honey for each chicken.

Waltur just had to know
how many chickens he had.
"Matilda," he said, "please count
my chickens for me."

Matilda rubbed her snout.
She went into
the backyard.

She came back inside.
"One," she said.

"What?" said Waltur.
"One," said Matilda.
"You have one chicken.
It is sitting on the eggs."

"No!" shouted Waltur.
"I have more than one chicken!
I have lots and lots of them!"

"Those are *eggs*," Matilda said.
"They are not chickens."

"But the eggs will become chickens,"
 said Waltur.

"Things can go wrong," said Matilda.
"A fox might eat the eggs.
 Or the eggs might be too cold to hatch."

"Never!" shouted Waltur.

3
Waltur and the Hen

Waltur stood in the backyard.
He looked at the bottom of the fence.
"A fox might try to sneak under the fence,"
he said.
"I will fix that fox."

Waltur pushed dirt up against the fence.

"There!" he said.
"No fox will be able to sneak
under the fence now."
"*Cluck*," said the hen.

Waltur looked at the top of the fence.
"I'll fix that fox," he said.

He pulled up sharp brambles.
"Ouch, ouch, ouch!" said Waltur.

He piled the brambles along the fence.
"There!" he said.
"No fox will be able to get over the fence now."
"Cluck," said the hen.

Waltur lay down next to the hen.
"I will help you," he said.
"I will stay here until the chickens hatch."
"Cluck," said the hen.

4
The Eggs Hatch

One day, Waltur heard a sound.
"What's that?" he asked.
The hen moved off the nest.
The eggs were hatching!

Waltur watched.
The hen watched.
Matilda and Darwin watched.

Peck, peck, peck.
Crack!

The first baby stepped
out of its shell.
"Quack!"
Soon the second one
came out.
"Quack!"

Ten eggs hatched.
Ten baby ducks stood there.

Quack, quack, quack. Quack, quack, quack.

"Something is wrong," said Waltur.
"Something is very wrong."
He went inside his house.
The ducks followed him.

Waltur sat in the chair.
Some ducks sat in the chair.
Some sat on the floor with Darwin.
Some sat on Waltur.

"I don't have any chickens," Waltur said.
"That means I can't sell chickens.
 That means I can't buy honey," he said.

Waltur needed to walk.
Matilda and Darwin walked with him.
The baby ducks followed them.
The hen went home.

Waltur saw a goat.
The goat had a sign: I TRADE THINGS.
"Nice ducks," said the goat.

"Ducks are not chickens," said Waltur.

"*Baaa,*" said the goat.
"I don't trade for chickens."

"Oh," said Waltur.

"But I trade for ducks," said the goat.

"Really?" asked Waltur.
"What do you have to trade?"

"Honey," said the goat.

The three friends carried the honey jars home.
They ate honey for lunch.
Waltur stacked the rest of the jars on a shelf.
He did not count them.

WALTUR

LEADS A HORSE TO WATER

1
Waltur Digs Holes

Waltur carried two buckets.
He gave one to Matilda.
"Let's play a game," he said.

"Good," said Matilda.

"Good," said Waltur.
"We can put dirt in the buckets."

"Dirt?" asked Matilda.
"Yes, dirt," said Waltur.
"We are going to play Dig Holes."

"But I do not want to dig holes,"
said Matilda.
"I want to play Count Bugs."

"Bugs?" asked Waltur.
He scratched his fur.

"I want to play Dig Holes.
See," he said. "Like this."
Waltur dug a big hole.

Matilda looked at the hole.

"I don't like holes," she said.
"Holes are boring."

"But digging holes is fun," said Waltur.
"Everybody loves to dig holes."

"Not me," said Matilda.

"Digging holes is more fun
  than counting bugs," said Waltur.
"Holes are bigger.
  And holes are better," he said.
"Everyone should dig holes."

Waltur dug a round hole.
He dug a square hole.
He dug a deep hole.

He talked about digging.
He talked about dirt.
Waltur had a very good time.

2
Waltur Leads a Horse

When Waltur looked around, Matilda was
sitting on a bucket.
She yawned.
She closed her eyes.

"What is wrong?" asked Waltur.
"I gave you a bucket.
 Now you should dig a hole," he said.

"No," said Matilda.
"You can't make me do what I don't
 want to do," she said.
"You can lead a horse to water, but you can't
 make it drink."

"I can, too!" Waltur shouted.
"I can do anything.
 I can lead a horse to water
 and I can make it drink."

"I don't think so," said Matilda.

"Let's go," said Waltur.
"I don't think you understand," said Matilda.

Waltur and Matilda walked
until they saw a horse.
"Hello, horse," said Waltur.
"Hello, bear," said the horse.
"I'm going to lead you
to water," said Waltur.
"Sounds good,"
said the horse.

Waltur held the horse's reins.
He led the horse a long way.
At last, Waltur, Matilda, and
the horse reached the river.

3
The Horse Will Not Drink

"Here's the water," said Waltur.
"So it is," said the horse.
"I led you here," said Waltur.
"Many thanks," said the horse.

"Now you can drink the water," said Waltur.
"Thank you, but no," said the horse.
"Yes," said Waltur. "Drink the water."
"No," said the horse. "I will not."

"Why not?" asked Waltur.
"I don't feel like it," said the horse.

"Water is good for you," said Waltur.
"So it is," said the horse.
"Drink the water," said Waltur.
"You drink it," said the horse.

"But I don't want any water," said Waltur.
"Neither do I," said the horse.
"I can make you drink the water," said Waltur.
"I think not," said the horse.

"*Grrrrr,*" growled Waltur.
"*Snort,*" snorted the horse.

Waltur stood behind the horse and pushed.
The horse sat down.
"Want to go for a ride?" asked the horse.
"No!" shouted Waltur.

Waltur stood in front of the horse
and pulled.
The horse backed up.
The reins snapped and Waltur fell
into the river.
The horse trotted away.

Matilda helped Waltur out of the river.
"You can lead a horse to water," she said.
"But you can't make it drink."
"I guess not," said Waltur.

4
Waltur
Thinks Hard

Waltur went home to think.
He thought for one full day.

The next day, Waltur had
a plan.
"Let's go find the horse,"
he said.
"Okay," said Matilda.

They found the horse.
"Hello again," said Waltur.
"Hello again," said the horse.
"I am going to lead you
to water," said Waltur.
"Sounds good," said the horse.

Waltur led the horse
to the river.

"I will not try to make you
  drink the water," said Waltur.
"That's good," said the horse.
"And I will not try to make
  Matilda dig holes," said Waltur.
"That's good," said Matilda.

"Let's play," said Waltur.
"What can we all play together?"

The horse thought hard.
"We could play Jump over Things,"
  said the horse.

Matilda thought hard.
"We could play Count Bugs," she said.

Waltur thought hard.
He thought very hard.

At last, Waltur had an idea.
"Let's play Waltur Digs Holes," he said.
"And let's play Matilda Counts Bugs in the Holes.
And let's play Horse Jumps over the Holes.
Let's play them all at the same time."

"That is a good idea," said the horse.
"Yes, that is a good idea," said Matilda.

So Waltur dug many, many holes.
"This is fun!" said Waltur.
"Please count the bugs," he said to Matilda.

Matilda counted all the bugs.
"This is fun," said Matilda.
"Please dig more holes," she said to Waltur.

The horse jumped over every hole.
"More holes, please," said the horse.

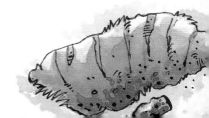

The horse jumped over every pile of dirt.
"More dirt, please," said the horse.

The horse even jumped over Waltur
and Matilda.

And then the horse drank some water.
Because it wanted to.

The End

FUNNY ENGLiSH SAYiNGS

From the beginnings of language, people have
loved to play with words.

An idiom is an example of words at play. It is
an old saying that has become part of the
language. An idiom means something bigger
than what it says — it expresses truths about
life. That is why idioms remain part of a
language for hundreds of years.

Don't buy a pig in a poke — This saying comes from five hundred years ago, when English farmers sold baby pigs in pokes, or bags. Some farmers put a cat inside the bag, not a pig. A person who bought a pig in a poke without first looking inside ended up being cheated.

Don't count your chickens before they're hatched — More than two thousand years ago the Greek storyteller Aesop told about a milkmaid who planned to get rich by selling eggs. But she couldn't buy the eggs, so she didn't become rich. Around the year 1500, people in England made up this saying from Aesop's story.

You can lead a horse to water, but you can't make it drink — This nine-hundred-year-old saying was probably made up by horse handlers who took horses to water each morning and then had to wait around until the horses were ready to drink.